Max and Zoe

at the Doctor

by Shelley Swanson Sateren

illustrated by Mary Sullivan

PICTURE WINDOW BOOKS

a capstone imprint

To Randall and Ruby, the original Banana Splits!

Max and Zoe is published by Picture Window Books
a Capstone Imprint
151 Good Counsel Drive, P.O. Box 669
Mankato, Minnesota 56002
www.capstonepub.com

Library of Congress Cataloging-in-Publication Data
Sateren, Shelley Swanson.
 Max and Zoe at the doctor / by Shelley Swanson Sateren ; illustrated
by Mary Sullivan.
    p. cm. -- (Max and Zoe)
 Summary: While practicing gymnastics with his friend Zoe, Max cuts
his leg and must get stitches.
 ISBN 978-1-4048-6212-8 (library binding)
 [1. Medical care--Fiction. 2. Gymnastics--Fiction. 3. Friendship--
Fiction.] I. Sullivan, Mary, 1958- ill. II. Title.
 PZ7.S249155Mat 2011
 [E]--dc22
                                        2011006483

Art Director: Kay Fraser
Designer: Emily Harris

Printed in the United States of America in Melrose Park, Illinois.

032011   006112LKF11

Table of Contents

Max and Zoe were at the city park.

"We need to practice our gymnastics," said Max.

"I know," said Zoe. "We have class tomorrow."

Zoe did a cartwheel and a headstand. Max did a round-off. He

landed in an excellent split.

"Wow!" said Zoe. "Did
that hurt?"

"Not at all," Max said.
"You try."

Zoe did a round-off. She
landed in an excellent split.

"We should start a club, Zoe," said Max. "Our club could be called The Banana Splits!"

"Cool!" said Zoe.

Max and Zoe did split after split.

"Wow!" said a boy. "Does that hurt?"

"Not at all," Max said.

"Max and Zoe!" called Mom. "Time to go."

"Yay!" Max yelled. "Time for ice cream!"

Max was so excited! He jumped on the rock wall. He did a cartwheel, right on top! Suddenly, Max's hand slid off the wall.

He fell toward the grass.

His leg hit a sharp rock.

"Ouch!" yelled Max.

"Oh no!" said Zoe. "You cut your leg."

"Now that hurts," said Max.

"That's a bad cut," said
Mom. "You need to see a
doctor. Ice cream will have
to wait."

"Will Max need stitches?"
Zoe asked.

"I don't know," said Mom.

"I got stitches on my chin once," said Zoe. "The doctor sewed the cut together."

Max had seen Zoe's grandma sew. The needle was sharp.

"I don't want stitches!" Max said.

Chapter 2
Is It Over Yet?

At the clinic, Max sat on

a table. Mom held his hand.

"You do need stitches,"

said the doctor. He cleaned

around the cut. "I'll give you

a shot. Then you won't feel

the pain."

The shot was over quickly.
The doctor washed the cut
with water. He wiped out
the dirt.

That part didn't hurt. But
would the stitches?

The doctor put some thread into a needle.

"Oh no," said Max.

"Don't look," said Zoe. "Watch me!"

Zoe did a split. Max watched.

"Wow!" said a nurse.

"When will it be over?"

asked Max.

"Soon," said the doctor.

Zoe did a headstand. Max watched.

"Is it over yet?" he asked.

"Almost," said the doctor.

Zoe's legs stayed up and up and up!

"That's your longest headstand ever!" said Max.

"We're done," said the doctor. "Seven stitches."

"It's done!" Max said.

"Good!" Zoe's legs dropped at last.

Chapter 3
Time for Ice Cream

Care Instructions for Stitches

1. No Swimming ☑
2. No Baths ☑

"Your stitches come out in one week," said the nurse. "Until then, keep your leg dry. No swimming."

"Shoot," Max said with a frown.

"And no baths," the nurse said.

"Great!" Max said with a smile. "Now it's time for ice cream!"

At the ice-cream shop,

Max was tired but hungry.

Max said to the worker,

"I got seven stitches!"

"Wow!" said the worker.

"That calls for a special

treat."

Max pointed at a sign.

"That's what I want."

"Me, too!" said Zoe.

"Banana splits!" they yelled together.

"You split your chin open," said Max. "I split my leg. We really are The Banana Splits!"

"A perfect ending to a crazy day," Zoe said.

About the Author

Shelley Swanson Sateren is the author of many children's books and has worked as an editor and a bookseller. Today, besides writing, she works with children aged five to twelve in an after-school program. At home or at the cabin, Shelley loves to read, watch movies, cross-country ski, and walk. She lives in St. Paul, Minnesota, with her husband and two sons.

About the Illustrator

Mary Sullivan has been drawing and writing her whole life, which has mostly been spent in Texas. She earned her BFA from the University of Texas in Studio Art, but she considers herself a self-trained illustrator. Mary lives in Cedar Park, a suburb of Austin, Texas.

Glossary

cartwheel (KART-weel) — a sideways flip with arms and legs held straight out

headstand (HED-stand) — holding yourself upright on your head with the help of your hands

round-off (ROUND-awf) — an act similar to a cartwheel that ends with both legs finishing together at the same time

splits (SPLITS) — to slide to the floor with your legs spread in opposite directions

stitches (STIH-chiz) — a way to close up a wound

Discussion Questions

1. Would you want to be in gymnastics? Why or why not?

2. Why is it important to go to the doctor if you are hurt?

3. Zoe helps distract Max while he's at the doctor. If you had to go to the doctor, who would you want to go with you? Why?

Hi MAX!

Writing Prompts

1. Max and Zoe name their club The Banana Splits. Make up your own club and make a poster for it. Be sure to include your club's name and its purpose.

2. It's important to stay safe when you are playing. Make a list of three playground rules.

3. Zoe is a good friend to Max. Write a few sentences about one of your good friends.

Make Your Own Banana Split

What you need:
- butter knife
- cutting board
- spoon
- ice cream scoop
- long bowl or a deep, oval dish
- 1 scoop each of vanilla, chocolate, and strawberry ice cream
- one banana
- sprinkles
- chocolate syrup
- strawberry ice-cream topping or fresh strawberries
- crushed nuts
- whipped cream
- 3 cherries

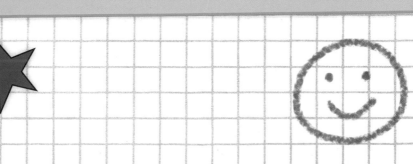

What you do:

1. Put one scoop of each flavor ice cream in the bowl or dish.

2. Peel the banana. With adult help, slice the banana in half the long way.

3. Press the "split" banana halves onto each side of the ice-cream row.

4. Top the vanilla ice cream with the sprinkles.

5. Top the chocolate ice cream with the chocolate syrup.

6. Top the strawberry ice cream with strawberry sauce or fresh strawberries.

7. Cover all of the scoops of ice cream with crushed nuts.

8. Top each scoop with some whipped cream.

9. Put a cherry on top of each scoop.

Now enjoy your tasty treat!

The Fun Doesn't Stop Here!

Discover more at www.capstonekids.com

- Videos & Contests
- Games & Puzzles
- Friends & Favorites
- Authors & Illustrators

Find cool websites and more books like this one at www.facthound.com. Just type in the Book ID **9781404862128** and you're ready to go!